PUFFIN BOOKS

Stardust
LUCY'S MAGIC JOURNAL

Linda Chapman lives in Leicestershire with her family and a Bernese mountain dog. When she is not writing she spends her time looking after her two daughters and baby son, horse riding and teaching drama.

Books by Linda Chapman

BRIGHT LIGHTS

CENTRE STAGE

NOT QUITE A MERMAID series

MY SECRET UNICORN series

STARDUST series

UNICORN SCHOOL series

Stardust

LUCY'S MAGIC JOURNAL

Linda Chapman

Illustrated by Angie Thompson

PUFFIN

PUFFIN BOOKS

Published by the Penguin Group
Penguin Books Ltd, 80 Strand, London WC2R ORL, England
Penguin Group (USA) Inc., 375 Hudson Street, New York, New York 10014, USA
Penguin Group (Canada), 90 Eglinton Avenue East, Suite 700, Toronto, Ontario, Canada M4P 2Y3
(a division of Pearson Penguin Canada Inc.)
Penguin Ireland, 25 St Stephen's Green, Dublin 2, Ireland (a division of Penguin Books Ltd)
Penguin Group (Australia), 250 Camberwell Road, Camberwell, Victoria 3124, Australia
(a division of Pearson Australia Group Pty Ltd)
Penguin Books India Pvt Ltd, 11 Community Centre, Panchsheel Park, New Delhi – 110 017, India
Penguin Group (NZ), 67 Apollo Drive, Rosedale, North Shore 0632, New Zealand
(a division of Pearson New Zealand Ltd)
Penguin Books (South Africa) (Pty) Ltd, 24 Sturdee Avenue, Rosebank, Johannesburg 2196,
South Africa

Penguin Books Ltd, Registered Offices: 80 Strand, London WC2R ORL, England

puffinbooks.com

First published 2008
1

Text copyright © Linda Chapman, 2008
Illustrations copyright © Angie Thompson, 2008
All rights reserved

The moral right of the author and illustrator has been asserted

Set in Monotype Bembo
Typeset by Palimpsest Book Production Limited,
Grangemouth, Stirlingshire
Made and printed in England by Clays Ltd, St Ives plc

British Library Cataloguing in Publication Data
A CIP catalogue record for this book is available from the British Library

ISBN: 978-0-141-32327-5

www.greenpenguin.co.uk

Mixed Sources
Product group from well-managed
forests and other controlled sources
www.fsc.org Cert no. SA-COC-1592
© 1996 Forest Stewardship Council

Penguin Books is committed to a sustainable future
for our business, our readers and our planet.
The book in your hands is made from paper
certified by the Forest Stewardship Council.

To Anna Joseph,
who would be one of Lucy's friends

Hi!

My name is Lucy Evans. I'm ten years old and this diary is all about me and my friends and our secret stardust spirit lives! If you don't know what a stardust spirit is, don't worry. I'd never heard about them either until my best friend, Allegra, moved in next door just over a year ago.

The very first day we met, Allegra told me that while all people are made of stardust, some people have more stardust than others. You can usually tell a stardust spirit from everybody else because they are extra-imaginative and they really love animals and believe in magic. Xanthe, she's Allegra's mum and a stardust spirit too (I'll tell you more about her later), also thinks that these special people have a glow about them. The important

I

*thing is that people who have the extra
stardust can turn into stardust spirits at night
time. It's amazing. When you are a stardust
spirit you can fly and do magic. There are four
types of stardust spirit – summer, autumn,
winter and spring – and we can all do
different kinds of magic.*

*I was so happy when I discovered I was a
stardust spirit too, although it's not just all
about having fun and flying around. You have
to look after nature – plants and animals.
Humans do all kinds of dumb things and if
you're a stardust spirit you have to put things
right. It can be something as small as helping
a vole who's got caught in a tin can or as big
as stopping a forest fire. Sometimes it's not
normal humans who cause the problems but
dark spirits – stardust spirits who have turned
bad and who use magic for themselves, not to*

help nature. They're very dangerous and scary and have to be stopped.

As for my non-stardust life, well, I'm just normal. I live in a village in Devon with my mum (Carol), my dad (Robert), my sisters (Rachel and Hope) who are thirteen and fourteen and my rabbit called Thumper who is so cute. I love him! My mum and dad are both quite strict. My dad loves animals and nature like me. As for my sisters, Rachel is really annoying, she's always teasing me, but Hope's nice. They both go horse riding lots. We live in a cottage called Jasmine Cottage and I go to the school in the village.

Our house is just on the edge of the village and has quite a big garden. On one side of it is Lavender Cottage and on the other side is Willow Cottage – where Allegra and Xanthe live. It's great living next door to Allegra because it means we get to have loads of sleepovers and spend all day together in the holidays. How cool is that?!

Anyway, I hope you enjoy reading this diary and learning all about my stardust world – maybe you'll discover that you're already part of it too!

Love,

Lucy xxx

Monday 10.00 a.m.

I think I'll start the diary by telling you a bit about me and my friends. We're all very different but that's what makes our adventures even more fun!

My Stardust Friends

Allegra Greenwood

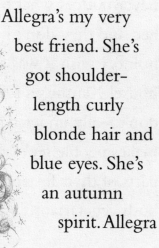

Allegra's my very best friend. She's got shoulder-length curly blonde hair and blue eyes. She's an autumn spirit. Allegra always has brilliant ideas but doesn't like being told what to do. Her mum, Xanthe, is a really powerful stardust spirit – she was once almost a dark spirit but not many people know that. She's got long blonde hair and is young for a mum. Allegra calls her Xanthe and not Mum, so it sometimes feels she's more like a big sister. Allegra and Xanthe never see Allegra's dad. Xanthe is really cool. She never notices what time Allegra goes to bed and they don't have many rules at home. I wish it was the same in my house! Xanthe's a reflexologist which I don't really understand but she says she makes people feel better by pressing on parts of their feet. She and Allegra are both vegetarians.

Ella Black

Ella is tall with
brown eyes and
long dark hair
that she ties back
in a ponytail.
She's a spring
spirit. She and
Faye are best
friends. They live
in the same town but not next door to
each other like me and Allegra although
they do go to school together. Ella's an
only child. She's very sensible and
responsible but good fun. She and Allegra
sometimes argue because Allegra always
wants to do things she shouldn't and Ella
wants to be good.

Faye Dawkins

Faye is small
with short fair
hair, big blue
eyes and a pixie-
ish face. She's a
winter spirit.
She's definitely
the quiet one
out of all of us.

She hates arguments. She's a really good
friend though and she always under-
stands if you're upset or unhappy. She's
got a younger sister, Lizzie, who really
annoys her. Lizzie is eight and has just
become a stardust spirit herself. Faye is
not happy at all! Poor Faye. I think I
would just die if Rachel became a
stardust spirit!

Robyn Jackson

Robyn's a new friend. She only moved into the area and joined our stardust group a few months ago but we're  really good friends with her now. Her mum, Joanna, is a summer spirit and was best friends with Xanthe when they were growing up. Robyn's got long dark hair that she usually straightens, and green eyes. She wears really cool clothes and is very popular. She's a summer spirit like me. I really like her.

And me

It feels weird
describing myself!
I'm normal
height, but a
bit more tall
rather than
small. I've got
long wavy
hair that's the
colour of a

conker. I've got greeny-grey eyes and a
round face. I guess I can be a bit bossy. I
like organizing things. The big thing to
know about me is that until recently my
powers were stronger than those of any
other spirit of my age; in fact I was
stronger than most of the adult spirits. It's
because I was the Last of the Summer

Spirits (I'll tell you about that later on!).

Now I'm not as powerful but I know
that the important thing about being a
stardust spirit is using the powers that
you do have as best you can to make
only good things happen and to work
together with your friends. And mine are
the best!

First Things First: How to Turn Into a Stardust Spirit

To turn into a stardust spirit, all you have
to do is stand in the starlight and say 'I
believe in stardust' three times. But there
are two important things to remember.
You have to really believe in what you're
saying and also the first time you say it
the stars have to be in certain places. I
didn't realize at first because Allegra and

Xanthe knew the stars were right when I tried for the first time. The planet Venus has to be passing through one of four signs of the Zodiac – Leo, Scorpio, Aquarius or Taurus. Xanthe says anyone who is a true stardust spirit will believe in magic so much that they will keep trying until one day they are lucky and the stars will be right. I know I would!

The Different Types of Stardust Spirits

There are four different types of stardust spirit – spring, summer, autumn and winter. Each type of spirit wears different-coloured clothes. Spring spirits wear green, summer spirits wear gold, autumn spirits wear silver and winter spirits wear blue. When someone turns

into a stardust spirit for the first time
they don't know what type of spirit they
are and their clothes are a pearly-grey
until they find out. It took me a while to
find out that I was a summer spirit. It's
really easy for some people though, they
seem to just know. Faye says she just
looked at the sky and felt drawn to
Aquarius. Allegra says she always knew
because if she shut her eyes she would
always see a picture of the Scorpion in
her mind. Ella took three weeks to find
out. I can't imagine that. It took me
about a week and that felt like ages!

The Royal Stars

Each different type of stardust spirit gets
their stardust from one of the Royal Stars
– the four brightest stars in the sky. Each

Royal Star is part of a group or constellation of stars that makes a picture in the sky. Aldebaran, the spring star, is part of the Bull; Regulus, the summer star, is part of the Lion; Antares, the autumn star, is part of the Scorpion; and Fomalhaut, the winter star, is part of the Water Bearer. The stars allow each different type of stardust spirit to do a different type of magic. There are two types of magic – basic magic and higher magic.

Xanthe also says that different types of spirits have different personality strengths and weaknesses. Looking at me and my friends, I think she's right.

I've drawn it all in a table to try and make it easier to understand.

I really think the personality thing is

right. I guess I am impetuous, which means rushing into things without thinking, and I do lose my temper sometimes. Not all the time though! Allegra's certainly easily bored but she has great ideas, Faye's very sensitive and Ella's very practical but also very stubborn. I remember Allegra and I talked to Xanthe about it once and she said that people always have good and bad sides to their personality and the two sides are linked. So Ella's very stubborn but that stubbornness also makes her very determined. And Faye gets upset easily because she is so sensitive but that also means that she is really sensitive when other people are unhappy. It's weird to think that you can't have the good

TYPE OF SPIRIT	ROYAL STAR	PERSONALITY (Strengths)
SUMMER (Me!)	Regulus The Lion	A Leader Brave Powerful
AUTUMN (Allegra)	Antares The Scorpion	Clever Adventurous Quick-thinking
WINTER (Faye)	Formalhaut The Water Bearer	Intuitive Fair-minded Creative
SPRING (Ella)	Aldebaran The Bull	Loyal Determind Practical

PERSONALITY (Weaknesses)	BASIC POWERS	HIGHER POWERS
Hot-tempered Impetuous Ambitious	Heating up and making fires	Creating magical shields
Easily bored Thoughtless	Summoning winds	Reading hearts and minds
Indecisive Over-sensitive	Summoning rain, snow and ice	Healing
Unadventurous Stubborn	Making things grow	Using magical disguises

without the bad. But nature's a bit like that – it's all about balance. And that's why, when I stopped being the Last of the Summer Spirits, I realized everything was still going to be OK ...

The Prophecy of the Last of the Summer Spirits

When the Last of the Summer Spirits is found,
Dark will fight light on the wooded ground.
Her strength is great and growing each day,
But true power comes when it's taken away.
When she gives up her stardust to the midnight sky
Four stars will unite and power will fly.

This prophecy was found in the stars by some adult stardust spirits and it turned out to be about me! When I first turned into a summer spirit there was a group of dark spirits trying to make themselves more powerful by interfering with the stardust in the sky. They were drawing down power from Regulus, the star that all the summer spirits' stardust comes from. This disrupted things so after I became a stardust spirit, there were no more summer spirits. Usually when someone turns into a spirit for the first time, power flows into them from their Royal Star until another new spirit comes along and then that new spirit gets the power but because there were no new summer spirits after me, I got more and more power. I could do all sorts of things I shouldn't have been able to do at my age, like using magic to stop things falling from the sky and being able to travel in an animal's mind. It was cool but then Xanthe realized that the reason I could do things like that was because I was the Last of the Summer Spirits. She told me about the prophecy. It was scary – even scarier when it really did come true. A few weeks ago there was a big battle between dark and light spirits. It's too long to tell you all about it now but thankfully we won. I did lose a lot of my extra powers but because of something Allegra, Ella, Faye and Robyn did, I actually gained some powers too. Now I am the only stardust spirit who can use all four types of stardust magic – winter, spring, summer and autumn. I'm

not very good at using my new powers
yet though. Things always seem to go
wrong! But I'm going to keep
practising!

Tuesday 5.00 p.m.

Hi there!

This is going to be a really quick diary
entry because I've got to get packed.
Faye, Ella and I are going round to
Allegra's for a sleepover tonight. Robyn
can't come because she's visiting her
cousins right now. We're going to make
Allegra's special fairy lemonade and have
a midnight feast. It's going to be brilliant
and . . . oh, hang on a minute, Mum's
calling me, back in a sec . . .

Back again! Mum just wanted to ask me
if I'd seen the Whites' young tabby cat,
Matilda. The Whites live just down the

road from us and they haven't seen
Matilda since yesterday. Mum said they
are getting very worried. I'll ask Allegra
tonight. Maybe she's seen her. I bet
Poppy White, who's four, will be really
sad; she really loves Matilda. She loves all
animals. Maybe she's going to be a
stardust spirit one day! Well, I'd better get
my things now. I'll write more later
when I'm at the sleepover!

Tuesday 11.00 p.m.

We're having such a fun time! Allegra,
Faye and Ella are playing Consequences
now while I write down what we've
been doing. This is what's happened so
far tonight.

After packing my rucksack – not
forgetting the sweets for the midnight
feast of course – I went round to
Allegra's. Just as I was about to knock on
the front door I saw the Whites – Liz,
Andy and their little girl, Poppy –
walking past towards their house.

'Hi!' I called. 'Have you found Matilda
yet?'

'No.' Liz looked worried. 'We've been

looking everywhere for her. It's so unlike her to stay out for a whole day and night.'

'Where is she, Mummy?' Poppy said. 'I want her to come home.'

'She will, sweetheart,' her dad, Andy, said.

'Yes, we'll find her,' Liz added quickly as Poppy's lower lip started to tremble. She scooped the little girl up. 'Don't worry.'

They carried on their way and I knocked on Allegra's door.

Allegra answered. 'Hi, Luce!' She frowned as she saw my face. 'What's up?'

'Matilda's missing,' I said. 'You know, the Whites' cat? You haven't seen her today have you?'

'No.' Allegra looked worried. 'I bet Poppy's upset.'

'She is,' I said. 'I hope they find her soon and that she's OK.'

'It would be awful if she was hurt or something,' Allegra said.

I shivered. 'Don't say that. Hopefully she's just got herself locked in someone's shed or garage. She's very nosy and always going in places she shouldn't.'

'Maybe we could help them look for her tomorrow if she still hasn't turned up?' Allegra suggested.

I nodded and we went upstairs.

Faye and Ella were sitting on Allegra's bed. Three camp beds had been set out next to it. I saw Faye's pink sleeping bag on one bed and Ella's turquoise sleeping bag with its cute dolphin print on the other bed.

'Hi, Lucy. Have you bought anything

for the midnight feast?' Faye asked.

I unzipped my rucksack and pulled out the big bag of sweets I'd bought from the newsagents. I'd got a load of flying saucers, some pink shrimps, some jelly strawberries and tiny teddy bears.

The others got out their things too. Ella had brought some crisps, Faye had

some chocolate and Allegra had a giant
bag of Maltesers.

'Cool!' Allegra said. 'We've got loads.
Let's divide everything up.'

After we'd split all the food into four
piles, we went to the kitchen to make
some of Allegra's special fairy lemonade.

If you want to make it this is what you
will need:

Some lemonade
Blackcurrant juice
Cranberry juice
Elderflower cordial
Ice cream
Sugar stars

You fill a jug with lemonade and then
add three big spoonfuls of the

blackcurrant juice, two big spoonfuls of
the cranberry juice and two big
spoonfuls of the elderflower cordial. Then
you add a big spoonful of ice cream, give
it a stir, pour it into glasses and sprinkle
the sugar stars on top of each glass. You
have to be careful though because it
sometimes fizzes up!

While Faye and I mixed the lemonade,
blackcurrant, cranberry and elderflower
in a jug and then poured it into glasses,
Allegra and Ella got the ice cream out of
the freezer.

'I wonder what it would taste like with
chocolate ice cream instead of vanilla,'
Allegra said. 'Let's try.'

'No,' Ella said quickly. 'It'll ruin it!'

'It might not,' argued Allegra.

'I'll try,' I offered, holding out my glass.

Allegra added a dollop of chocolate ice cream. It fizzed slightly and started to melt. Faye giggled. 'It looks like poo!'

'I hope it doesn't taste like that.' I took a cautious sip. It wasn't bad. 'Actually it's quite nice.' There was a sugar bowl in the middle of the table with a spoon in it. I had an idea. 'I wonder what it'll be like with some sugar!' I said, adding a big spoonful.

Allegra gasped, her hand flying to her mouth.

'What?' I said suspiciously.

'Nothing,' she said, her blue eyes suddenly wide and innocent.

The mixture frothed up. I lifted the glass, took a gulp and immediately spat it out. 'Yuck!' I exclaimed.

Allegra burst out laughing. 'That wasn't sugar, Luce! That was salt!'

'Gross!' I wailed. 'You could have told me!'

'Why?' Allegra grinned. 'It was much funnier to watch you drink it!'

I grabbed the vanilla ice cream from the table, scooped up a spoonful and flicked it at her. It landed directly on her nose. She squealed in surprise.

Faye, Ella and I all giggled.

'Right!' Allegra exclaimed and grabbing the chocolate ice-cream container she picked up an enormous spoonful and raised her arm.

'No, don't, don't!' I gasped.

Allegra moved her arm as if to fire it at me but just as I tensed, she put the spoon down.

I breathed out in relief.

'Mmm, tasty!' Allegra said, sticking her tongue out and licking the ice cream.

After we had made some more fairy lemonade – with vanilla ice cream this time – we helped Xanthe get supper ready. It was cheese and tomato pizza and

salad. We took it outside on to the
decking in the garden to eat. It was lovely
sitting outside, watching the sun set and
munching on our pizza.

Afterwards we went upstairs to
Allegra's room and got into our pyjamas.

'Let's have our midnight feast,' I said.
'After all, we won't be here at midnight
because we'll be in the woods!'

We had decided to turn into stardust
spirits as soon as it was properly dark.
While we had been eating supper,
Xanthe had told us that a pair of
firecrests had been spotted in the conifers
to the east of the woods. Firecrests are
tiny, very rare birds. Xanthe wanted us to
check out the conifers that night to see if
we could find out if they were nesting in
the woods or just passing through.

We all got into our pyjamas. Then we got into our sleeping bags, not to sleep but just because it was cosy. 'What shall we do while we wait for it to get dark?' Allegra said.

'Why don't we tell ghost stories?' I suggested. I *love* ghost stories!

'Yeah!' said Ella.

Faye looked worried. 'I don't really like ghost stories.'

'Ghosts aren't real,' said Ella.

'Oh yes they are!' said Allegra. 'Wait till I tell you my story!' She jumped up, switched off the lights and got back into her sleeping bag. 'OK, I'll start,' she said, lowering her voice. 'When my gran was eighteen she was working in a hotel. She lived there with the other staff. It was a really old building and she said that there was a ghost that haunted it. It was said to be the ghost of the lady who had once owned it. One night my gran had to stay in a different room and she was put in the oldest part of the house. She was in bed and she woke up and saw this person standing beside her bed looking at her. It was an old lady dressed in a long white dress with a shawl around her shoulders. She was carrying an oil lamp. My gran said she was so scared she couldn't move. The woman started walking straight towards her . . .'

'What happened?' Faye whispered.

'The lady came all the way over to the bed, touched my gran's head – Gran said it was like an ice cube – and then the lady walked away and walked straight through the wall and disappeared!'

'You're making it up!' said Ella.

'No, I'm not! I swear I'm not!' Allegra said. 'My gran told everyone. And guess what?'

'What?' Faye breathed as Allegra looked round at us all.

'It turned out that was the room the lady's daughter used to have as her bedroom. The wall hadn't been there then; it had only been put up a few years ago. It was like the old lady was checking on her daughter and then walking to the other side of the room!'

'Maybe it was just your gran dreaming,' I said glancing at Faye, who had her knees hugged tightly to her chest.

Allegra shook her head seriously. 'She says it really happened. I think it's very scary. I'd hate to see a ghost.'

'Why?' said Ella. 'Even if there are ghosts they never seem to hurt anyone. You never hear about anyone being killed by a ghost.'

'Or maybe we just never find out that they've been killed by a ghost,' Allegra said in a whisper.

Faye put her hands over her ears. 'Stop it! Stop it!'

I could see Faye was starting to get really upset. 'OK, let's stop now and do something else. Why don't we play Consequences?'

'It's almost time to turn into stardust spirits,' said Allegra, looking out of the window at the darkening sky.

'We could play Consequences while we wait,' said Ella.

Allegra found some paper and pens.

We all played one game and even Faye was soon laughing again as we read out the things we'd written.

They've started playing a third game of it now while I write this down. It's properly dark outside now and we're about to turn into stardust spirits. More later!

Wednesday 3.30 a.m.

Hi again!

We're back! The others have gone to bed
but I wanted to write down what we'd
been doing. We've had a brilliant night *and*
managed to make someone very happy!

When we got to the woods, we flew
to the secret clearing where all the
stardust spirits who come to our woods
meet every night. There were about
twenty spirits there.

Four stardust spirits, all a couple of
years younger than us, were playing tag.

'Oh,' Faye said, not sounding delighted.
'Lizzie's here.'

'Hi, Faye!' called a spirit with

shoulder-length blonde hair and a golden
dress. It was Faye's younger sister, Lizzie.
She had become a stardust spirit for the
first time a few weeks ago.

'Hi,' Faye said briefly. She and Lizzie
really don't get on.

Lizzie swooped over to us. 'Are you
having a good sleepover?' Although
she looks quite like Faye with her
heart-shaped face and big blue eyes, she
is much louder and not at all shy.

'Yes,' Faye turned to us. 'Let's go and
look for those firecrests.'

'Ooo! Firecrests! I'd like to see them!'
Lizzie said. 'Can we come?' Faye opened
her mouth to protest but Lizzie didn't
wait for her to answer. She swung round.
'Hey, guys!' she shouted to her friends –
Charlotte, Georgia and Isabella. 'Faye and

the others are going to see some firecrests. Let's go with them!'

They flew over.

'That sounds cool!' said Charlotte.

'Can we really come?' asked Georgia.

Allegra shrugged. I could see she felt she couldn't really say no. 'Sure.'

Faye's face fell.

However, just then Sarah, one of the adult spirits, flew over. 'Girls,' she said to the younger ones. 'Could you come with me, please? We want to start teaching you how to use your magic powers.'

'But we were going to look at the firecrests,' Lizzie protested.

Sarah smiled at her. 'You'll have to go another day, I'm afraid. Come on!'

Lizzie and the other three didn't have any choice but to follow her.

'Phew!' Faye breathed out. 'It's bad enough being with Lizzie at home without having to spend the nights with her! She always thinks she knows best even though I'm older than her and she *never* stops talking. She is *so* annoying!'

'Let's go and find the firecrests,' said Ella.

The conifers where the firecrests had been spotted were in a very quiet place, deep in the east of the woods. We didn't usually go there. There was always a slightly creepy feel to the air, the tall trees towered overhead and their evergreen leaves blocked out the light all year round.

We landed on the ground. There was a carpet of pine needles and pine cones. The air was very still and silent.

'So, what exactly do firecrests look like?' I asked, thinking that my voice sounded very loud in the silence.

'They're really small,' replied Allegra. She knew more about nature than any of us. 'They're one of the smallest birds in Europe. They've got lime-green feathers on their back and really brightly coloured heads, with an orangey-yellow stripe on the top of their head bordered by black stripes and then white markings above the eyes. They move really quickly but we probably won't see them now as they'll be sleeping. Xanthe wants to know if they are just roosting in a tree or if they have made a nest.'

'What type of nest should we look for?' Faye asked.

'It will be small, probably near the end of a branch and made out of moss and lichens,' Allegra explained.

'It's going to take us ages to check all these trees,' said Ella, looking round. 'We'd better split up.'

Faye looked round. 'Do we have to? It's really spooky here.'

'It'll be much quicker if we look on our own,' Ella pointed out.

A shiver ran across my skin. I could see why Faye was a bit nervous. The shadows all around us did look very creepy.

'Ella's right,' Allegra said. 'Let's split up and meet back here in fifteen minutes. OK?'

We set off into the trees. It was very dark and I had to peer through the gloom to check round the branches. My skin prickled. I couldn't hear the others at all. I suddenly had a horrible feeling that someone was watching me. I swung round. There was no one there.

You're being dumb, I told myself. *There's nothing to be scared of.*

CLUNK!

I jumped as I heard the strange noise

from the ground beneath me. It sounded
like someone hitting the trunk of a tree
with something hard!

I peered down. I couldn't see anything
through the darkness. Was there someone
there? But what would someone be
doing in the depths of the woods in the
middle of the night?

You must have imagined it, I told myself.
There wasn't really a noise . . .

CLUNK!

I *hadn't* imagined it! Images from
the ghost stories we had been listening
to earlier filled my mind. I got really
scared. Turning round, I raced back
to the clearing where I'd left the
others.

Faye was there. 'Lucy!' she said, looking
very relieved to see me. 'I'm so glad

you're back. I don't like being on my own. Can I fly with you?'

I took a breath and tried to calm down. Now I was out of the shadows it was easier to feel more sensible. A ghost really *couldn't* be making the noise. Ghosts just didn't exist.

'What's the matter?' Faye asked, seeing my face.

'I . . . I think there's someone in the trees,' I replied. 'There's a banging noise coming from the ground.'

'What shall we do?' Faye said in alarm.

I tried to be brave. It *had* to be a normal person, and if they were in the woods at this time of night then they had to be up to no good. We were stardust spirits; we were supposed to protect the animals and plants in the

woods. We had to find out what was
going on!

'Go and check it out. Come on!'

We flew deep into the trees swooping
round the tree trunks and ducking under
branches. 'The noise was coming from
somewhere near here,' I hissed, listening
hard. 'It's like a —'

YEEOOOOOWWWWOOOO!

A strange, muffled cry echoed up from
the ground. My heart somersaulted in my
chest. What was *that*?

YEEEOOOOOOWWWWOOOO!

The noise came again, echoey, sort of
hollow-sounding. No person on earth
could make that kind of noise. No living
person anyway!

'It's a ghost!' gasped Faye, looking
terrified.

She turned round and flew through the trees as fast as she could. I raced after her. We broke through the trees into the clearing just as Allegra came flying out of the trees.

She took one look at our faces and stared. 'What's up? You look like you've seen a ghost!'

'We have!' I gasped. 'Or at least not seen one but *heard* one.'

'Oh, Allegra, it's horrible,' Faye said, shooting a terrified look behind her. 'Quick! We've got to get out of here!'

'But –'

Allegra broke off as Ella came flying through the trees.

'Ella! Quick!' Faye cried. 'There's a ghost!'

'A ghost? Don't be stupid!' Ella started

to grin but the next moment the grin froze on her face.

CLUNK!

CLUNK!

The weird banging noise I'd heard before was coming through the trees towards us!

YYYYEEEEOOOOWWWWWW! A mournful cry echoed through the air.

'Let's get out of here!' Allegra gasped. Faye, Allegra and I turned and flew away as fast as we could.

As we reached the trees on the far side, I suddenly realized that Ella wasn't with us. I swung round. 'Ella! Come on!'

'It can't be a ghost!' she said practically, hands on hips. 'They don't exist!' She looked round.

My eyes caught a movement low to

the ground in the shadows of the trees.
Something was coming out from behind
them. All the hairs on my arms were
standing up.

Suddenly Ella pointed. 'Oh, goodness!
Look!' she cried, and she burst out
laughing.

I stared at her. She was *laughing*!

'There's your ghost,' she giggled.

Flying closer, I gasped. 'Oh!'

A tabby cat was walking out of the
trees with a large glass jar stuck on its
head and inside the jar was a mouse!

'Matilda!' I exclaimed.

Matilda opened her mouth and yowled
mournfully, the sound echoing in the glass
jar. So that had been our ghostly noise!
She shook her head from side to side,
clunking the jar into the trunk of a tree.

Just then, Faye and Allegra came flying back into the clearing.

'What's happening . . .?' Allegra broke off as she saw Matilda. 'Oh, poor thing!'

We all flew down and landed on the grass beside the unhappy cat. The little brown mouse inside the jar looked even more unhappy. It was stuck at the bottom of the jar only a few centimetres away from Matilda's nose.

'She must have been chasing the mouse and chased it into the jar!' Allegra said. 'Then got stuck!'

'Oh, you silly thing,' I murmured to the tabby. Matilda's collar was stopping her getting her head out because the buckle was catching on the rim of the glass. While Allegra held Matilda's body, I held the jar still and Faye worked her fingers inside the jar. She managed, after a few minutes, to unbuckle the collar. As it fell off Matilda's neck, Matilda pulled back, her head coming out of the jar. Allegra scooped her up. 'There, there,' she soothed. 'It's all right, you're free now.'

I gently tipped the jam jar upside down and the relieved mouse dashed out into my hands. It looked very scared and bewildered. I stroked its soft fur gently until it relaxed and then I put it down and it scampered safely away into the bushes. Matilda tried to leap out of Allegra's arms to chase after it but Allegra kept a tight hold. 'Oh no,' she said. 'You've done enough mousing for tonight. It's time for you to go home!'

Matilda gave in and settled back into Allegra's arms.

I stroked her head. 'Poppy will be so glad we've found you.'

'Can I have a cuddle?' Faye asked. As Allegra handed her over, Faye smiled. 'To think we thought you were a ghost.'

I felt rather embarrassed. 'Yeah. OK. That *was* a bit dumb.'

'A bit?' said Ella. She broke off as I threw a pine cone at her.

'Hey!' she exclaimed, ducking. She

grabbed one herself and threw it back at me. Allegra joined in. Soon there were pine cones whizzing everywhere and we were all shrieking. Faye flew out of the way with Matilda while Allegra and Ella and I chucked them at each other.

'Zi–zi–zi. Zi–zi–zi.'

From above us came the sound of a bird's alarmed call.

'Come on, you lot,' Faye called. 'You're going to wake up half the animals and birds in the woods if you carry on like this! Let's take Matilda back to her house.'

We flew up after her.

'Zi–zi–zi!'

I saw that a bird had popped out of a nest and was perched at the end of a branch – it was a tiny, green bird with

black and white feathers on its wings and
a bright yellowy-orange flash of colour
on its head.

'It's all right,' Allegra started to say to it
and then she broke off with a gasp. 'Hey,
it's a firecrest!'

We all looked at the little bird.

'It was right above us all the time!' Ella
exclaimed.

Another bird joined it. 'There's its mate!' I said.

'And they *are* nesting!' Allegra said. 'Xanthe will be so pleased!'

'There are eggs!' I said, looking into the nest and seeing seven small pale eggs. 'Oh wow!'

Allegra hugged me. 'This is brilliant! What a cool night! We've found the firecrests *and* we've found Matilda!'

I hugged her back. 'We should all have sleepovers together more often.'

'Every day,' Faye agreed happily.

Leaving the birds to settle back on their nest we flew out of the woods. As we reached the village we camouflaged ourselves so that no one could see us. I led the way into the Whites' garden. Poppy's curtains were open and I could see her in bed, clutching a fluffy brown cat toy. I smiled to myself. She would be so happy in the morning when she found Matilda!

We flew down. Luckily the back door had a cat flap in it. Faye opened it and Matilda miaowed and hopped through. It fell shut. We all breathed out in relief.

'She's safe home again!' said Allegra.

'Let's go back to the woods and tell Xanthe about the firecrests!' Ella said.

We raced back to the clearing. Xanthe was delighted to hear the news and put us in charge of watching over the tiny birds. We're all dying to see the firecrest eggs hatch out!

Afterwards we played tag and went to check on the badgers by the river before flying back to Allegra's.

The others have gone to sleep already but I wanted to write down what we have been doing. I'm tired now though and think I'd better go to sleep too. I'll write more tomorrow!

P.S. I hope I don't dream about ghosts!!

Wednesday 10.30 a.m.

Hi there!

Back home now. Allegra's coming round
after lunch and we're going to make an
obstacle course for my rabbit, Thumper.
He's got an orange harness that he wears
with a lead but he doesn't always go
where I want him to though! Until then
you should read this email I had waiting
for me when I got back from Allegra's.
It's from my friend Tess. Tess lives in
Pembrokeshire with her mum, Fran, and
her dad, David. They are all stardust
spirits and they're really good friends of
Xanthe and Allegra. Allegra and I went
to stay with them in the Easter holidays.

We hung round with Tess and her
friends Lottie and Bea. It was brilliant
fun apart from meeting Dan, a really
scary dark spirit. Anyway, here's Tess's
email:

Hi Lucy!

How are you? Everything's fine
here. Lottie and Bea said to say
hi. Guess what? The polecats that
live in the cliffs beneath
Carwyn's Rest have had six
babies, or kits, as my mum says
they're called. They are SO cute!
Lottie, Bea and I were flying over
the cliffs last night when we saw
the mum and dad come out of a
burrow with them. They're

gorgeous - loads of fluffy black
fur and tiny bright eyes. I wish
you could see them. You and
Allegra must come and visit again
soon! There are loads of seal
pups now as well and the grass
around Carwyn's Rest is still
growing. Do you remember that it
used to be just bare soil but
then, when we fought Dan, the
escaping magic hit the ground and
Bea made plants grow there? I bet
you do. I know I won't ever
forget it! Anyway, it's really
green now and the whole place
feels different. That creepy
feeling about the air has gone.
Me, Lottie and Bea camped out
there last week. It was cool! We

woke up in the morning just as
the sun was rising. When we got
up, we saw dolphins and seals in
the bay. You must come and stay
again SOON!!!

Lots of love,

Tess x

I wrote back:

Hi Tess,

Cool to hear from you. Say hi
back to Lottie and Bea for me.
It's been exciting here. We've
found some firecrests nesting in
the woods and we rescued a cat

called Matilda yesterday. She had
been chasing a mouse in the woods
that had run into a jam jar.
Matilda had put her head in and
got the jam jar stuck! We freed
her and took her home. I saw her
this morning. Her family are so
happy she's back. Poppy, the
little girl, couldn't stop
smiling and cuddling her. Poppy's
mum said Matilda ate a huge
breakfast and said they wondered
where she'd been. I would have
loved to tell them about the jam
jar and about finding her but of
course I had to keep quiet. Being
out in the woods in the middle of
the night would be a bit of a
hard one to explain! Anyway, I'm

just glad Matilda's safe. The
polecat kits sound very cute. I
wish I could see them - and the
seals and dolphins. I'm writing a
diary at the moment. I'm going to
put this email in. I hope you
don't mind. Mail again soon!

Lots of love,

L x

I would love to go and stay with Tess
again! The polecat kits sound gorgeous.
Anyway, for now I thought I'd tell you a
bit more about magic in the stardust
world.

Star Stones

Some stardust spirits believe that you can
increase your ability to do magic by
wearing a particular kind of crystal.
Each different type of stardust spirit has
a different type of crystal to use. Summer
spirits use onyx, a black and white stone;
autumn spirits use topaz, which is a gold
colour; winter spirits use amethyst, which

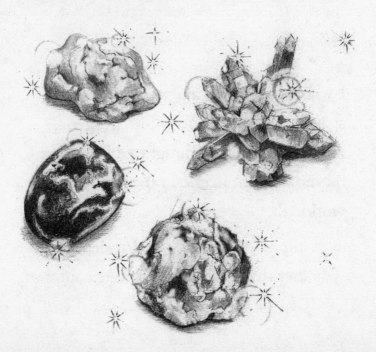

is purple; and spring spirits use turquoise, a bluey-green stone. I'm not sure I believe crystals really work. Xanthe says you find your magic inside you and I think she's right. I like wearing my star stone though. I have onyx earrings now, but at first I wasn't allowed to have my ears pierced and so had to wear my crystal on an ankle bracelet. Even though I've got earrings now, I still wear my ankle bracelet sometimes because Allegra and the others bought it for me and so it's special.

Deep Magic

All stardust spirits can fly and camouflage themselves so they appear to be invisible. They also all have basic magic powers and higher magic powers that depend on whether they are spring, summer, autumn

or winter spirits. But there are also extra
powers that only some stardust spirits
have, Xanthe says they are based on
much deeper ancient magic. Only a few
very powerful stardust spirits develop
them. I used to be able to use lots of
deep magic very easily when I was the
Last of the Summer Spirits but I can't
any more; however, Xanthe says she
thinks I'm powerful enough that I'll be
able to develop some of the deep powers
as I get older. These are some types of
deep magic that I know about:

Talking to animals

Some stardust spirits can talk to animals
with their thoughts. Xanthe can. I would
love to be able to. Xanthe has said that
she will teach me one day.

Stopping something falling through the air

I could do this when I was the Last of
the Summer Spirits. You look at
something – or someone – and stop
them falling. It's a bit like binding magic
if you do it to a person. I once did it to
Faye and she was really upset. I promised
I would never do it again.

Binding magic

This is when a stardust spirit keeps
another spirit captive with their mind;
the captured spirit can't move or speak.
It's really cruel and it's a type of magic
only used by dark spirits.

Travelling in an animal's mind

I also did this when I was the Last of the
Summer Spirits. I travelled with an otter
and a tawny owl. It's an amazing feeling.
You get to see through their eyes and
hear what they hear and their thoughts
flash through your brain. You are not
allowed to try and make the animal go
where you want to; you just sit lightly in
its mind, letting it take you where it
wants. Only dark spirits try and make an
animal do what they want.

Transforming into an animal

This is when you change into an animal
to spy on people or move around
unnoticed. Usually only dark spirits do
this although I saw Xanthe do it once,
but that was to save me.

They are all the types of deep magic that I know at the moment but I bet there are more. Oops, Mum is calling me for lunch. I'd better go! Bye for now!

Thursday 4.00 a.m.

Hi!

I've had a really fun night as a stardust spirit. Me, Allegra, Ella and Faye played magic hide-and-seek where we hide by camouflaging ourselves. Then we were sent to clear up a grove at the edge of a wood where some people had been having a campfire. The ground had been burnt and lots of plants trampled. There was litter all over the place. It makes me really mad that people can be so thoughtless.

We all cleared up the litter and then Ella set to work regrowing the plants. She asked me to help her. It was really

strange to be asked. I'm so used to only
doing one type of magic – my summer
spirit magic. But now it's different. Now
I can do all four types of magic and join
in with any of the others. I'm not much
help though. I'm fairly useless at doing
spring, autumn and winter magic at the
moment. When I tried to help Ella
regrow the grass and plants on the
burnt ground, I wanted to make grass
spring up but managed to make a
clump of giant sunflowers that were
about three metres high! Ella had to get
rid of them for me. After she'd made
the grass grow back, Faye conjured
some rain to water the clearing. I tried
to help but I just couldn't make a rain
cloud come. I'm useless at winter
magic.

It's strange trying to learn how to do different kinds of magic. Doing summer magic feels so easy and natural. I think what I want to do and I can do it. Power just rushes through me and I can make things burst into flame or heat up or protect them with a magical shield. It's much more difficult for me to do spring, winter and autumn magic. Each Royal Star's magic feels different. When I do summer magic, the power that rushes through me feels strong and fast and powerful, like a forest fire blazing inside me. But when I do spring magic, to make things grow, it's a much heavier feeling; it's like my feet are growing into the ground and as if power is flowing steadily into me from the earth. It's a solid, warm, almost safe

74

feeling. Autumn magic feels difficult to control. It whistles through me, blowing through my whole body; it's strong and hard to keep control of. I feel like it could burst out of me at any second and I have to really struggle to contain it but I like it because it gives me the same feeling of dangerous, huge power as summer magic. It feels scary as well as good. Winter magic is the most difficult for me. It doesn't rush into me; it just suddenly feels like it's there, in my whole body. It's hard to get hold of; the power's there but it always seems to slip away before I can do anything. I try to focus it and make it do what I want but it just disappears. I haven't made it rain once yet. Sometimes it feels like I've got so much to learn. I hope one day I'll be able to use all the different types of magic as easily as I use my summer magic. That will be so cool!

Bed now. I'll write more tomorrow. N'night.

Thursday 9.30 a.m.

Wow! I woke up to another email from Tess. She's been helping a stranded dolphin. I've put it in so you can read all about it:

Hi Lucy,

I just had to email you. I've had such a night. Bethan (one of the other adult spirits - do you remember her?) found a male bottlenose dolphin stranded in a small cove near the beach where we always meet. The tide had gone out and he was stuck on the sand. She came and told us and we all

raced to help him. Although
dolphins breathe air, their skin
needs to stay wet and so some of
the winter spirits conjured a
rain cloud over him. But then the
problem was how to get him back
into the water. He was really
frightened and thrashing his tail
about so we couldn't get near
enough to touch him. I know
dolphins are really friendly when
they're in the water (do you
remember flying with those
dolphins swimming beneath us when
you visited?) but when they are
on land they panic and if you are
too close they can really injure
you with their tails or by
throwing themselves about, so you

have to be really careful. We
needed to calm him down. Mum says
that Xanthe can talk to animals
but no one in our group of
stardust spirits can do that so
we couldn't soothe him that way.
He was panicking so much he
didn't seem to realize we were
stardust spirits and not normal
humans. Dad got everyone to back
off and then he got me, yes ME,
to go up closer! He said he
thought that if the dolphin just
saw a child rather than a load of
adults he would gradually stop
panicking and maybe realize that
we were stardust spirits and that
we were trying to help him.

I went close to the dolphin and

just talked and talked as
soothingly as I could. I can't
even remember half the things I
said but it gradually seemed to
work. The dolphin calmed down,
his eyes softened and he stopped
throwing himself about. When he
was still I went up to him, ready
to fly into the air at any moment
if he moved suddenly - but he
didn't. He let me stroke him. I
got drenched from the rain that
was falling but I didn't mind. I
just crouched down and stroked
his head. He looked at me with
his dark eyes and I could tell
somehow that he was saying 'help
me'.

'We will,' I promised him.

He seemed to relax. I kept
stroking him as Dad and the other
adults came closer. We knew we had
to get him back into the water as
soon as possible.

Luckily the tide had only just
started going out. Someone flew to
get some ropes and we managed to
get them underneath him. Then we
used them to lift him as gently as

we could and carry him to the
water. It took twenty people to
move him because he was really
heavy and we had to do it as
carefully as possible so that he
wouldn't start panicking again. I
talked to him the whole time and
he kept his eyes fixed on me.

We got him to the water but he
still wasn't safe. Dolphins suffer
land sickness like people get
seasick - if they are out of the
water for too long they lose their
sense of balance and can't swim
when you put them back into the
water. When we got him into the
sea we had to stay with him,
rocking him gently from side to
side. At first he didn't do

anything, it was like he was
frozen and had forgotten how to
swim but then he started to move
his flippers and suddenly he was
OK! With a flick of his tail he
plunged away from us. I was in the
water with Mum and Dad. Luckily
it's been a really hot day today
and the water was still warm. It
was amazing to watch him swim
away. He dived down into the water
and surfaced a little way off. He
turned and looked at us and opened
his mouth as if he was smiling.
Then he swam straight back.

'What's he doing?' Mum exclaimed
as he headed towards us and the
shore. 'He's going to strand
himself again.'

Everyone gasped but the dolphin didn't swim on to the beach, he swam up to me! He stopped in front of me and whistled softly. It was just like he was saying 'thank you'! I touched his head and he nudged me with his nose, whistled again and then he turned and raced away.

It was the best moment of my

whole life! To see him free again and swimming out to sea – it was just amazing! Mum and Dad hugged me and then we all went back to the beach and made a campfire. Oh, Lucy, I wish you and Allegra had been with us! Mum says dolphins have very good memories and she thinks he will come back and look for me. Wouldn't that be brilliant?

Better go now. Say hi to Allegra for me and tell her about my dolphin experience. Tell her to MAIL ME!!!!

Love,

Tess x

Isn't that an amazing story! I've got to show the email to Allegra. I wrote back quickly.

Hi Tess,

That's amazing. You must have been so relieved that he was OK and then to have him come back and see you like that. Wow! That is SO cool! I'm going to go and tell Allegra right now. Have a fun day!

L x

Thursday 12.30 p.m.

I went round to Allegra's and told her
about Tess and the dolphin. She thought
it was brilliant too and said she'll email
Tess about it. Allegra's useless at keeping
in touch with people. She always says she
will but then forgets. That's why Tess
usually emails me now. At least she knows
I'll reply! Allegra doesn't mind Tess
emailing me, even though she and Tess
have been friends much longer. Allegra
and Xanthe are going away tomorrow for
two nights. They're going to Dorset to
visit Xanthe's god-daughter, Chloe, who
has just moved there. Chloe's ten. Xanthe
hasn't seen her for a while but she thinks
she might be a stardust spirit. Allegra says

Chloe is really good fun — she loves animals. Allegra can't wait to find out if she is a stardust spirit. I wish Allegra wasn't going away but I guess she'll be back soon.

Friday 3.45 a.m.

I've got so much to tell you! It's been a very busy night and I even got to see an animal being born!

As soon as it got dark and Mum and Dad had gone to bed, I went to the woods with Allegra and Xanthe.

'What would you like us to do tonight?' I asked Xanthe, as we swooped into the trees.

'Two things really,' she replied. 'I'd like you to check the deer who roam on the west side of the wood. Find the herd and count how many stags, does and fawns there are and then can you come and find me because I would like to check the pregnant does and see that they're all looking healthy.'

'OK,' said Allegra. 'And what's the other thing?'

'I'd like you to help Lizzie, Charlotte, Georgia and Isabella. They've been learning about their magic with some of the adults for the last few nights but I think they're ready to start practising on their own now. However, they do need someone to keep an eye on them. Could you two and Ella and Faye help them out a bit?'

'Of course we can,' I said.

'Thanks,' said Xanthe. 'Just remember they won't be able to make their magic do exactly what they want yet. You'll have to be patient. Help them learn how to do it for themselves.'

We reached the main stardust clearing.

Stardust spirits were swooping through
the air and sitting in the branches of the
big oak tree in the centre of the clearing.
Georgia, Charlotte and Isabella were
already there. 'Hi!' I called. 'Xanthe's asked
us to help you practise your magic tonight.'

'Cool!' Charlotte said. 'So, there'll be
no adults with us?'

'No, just us,' I replied. 'When the others get here we can go to the aspen grove. It'll be quieter there.'

'And we can try and find the deer afterwards,' Allegra added to me. 'They usually roam through the woods near there.'

Just then Ella, Faye and Lizzie flew into the stardust clearing. 'Oh, come on, Faye, don't be boring!' Lizzie was saying. She swooped round and tagged her sister's arm. 'Tag!'

Faye looked irritated. 'Stop it, Lizzie! I said I don't want to play!'

'Tag!' Lizzie said, grinning and tagging her again and again.

Faye and Ella dived away and flew over to us.

'Let's get out of here,' said Faye.

'Lizzie's driving me mad! What are we supposed to be doing tonight?'

I had a feeling Faye wasn't going to like the answer. 'Um, helping Lizzie and the others practise their magic powers.'

'Oh no,' Faye groaned.

Lizzie came racing over. 'Hey! I've just heard that we're going to practise our magic with you guys tonight.' She spun round in the air. 'Come on then! Let's go and get started!'

We flew to the aspen grove; Lizzie was keen to be the first to practise her magic. She pointed at a twig. 'Fire be with me!'

The twig started to smoke.

'That's good,' I encouraged her. It wasn't a fire but I knew most young summer spirits found it very hard to start fires.

'Shall I show you what I can do?' asked Charlotte. We nodded and she called a breeze into the clearing. It swept through, whisking our hair back and making it hard to keep standing.

'Great,' Allegra gasped. 'Though it's a bit strong!'

'Sorry,' said Charlotte, 'I'm no good at controlling how strong the wind is.'

Next Georgia made it rain. She couldn't make the rain cloud go where she wanted though and we all had to shelter under the branches of an aspen tree until Faye made the cloud go away. Then Isabella tried to make a patch of buttercups grow, only they ended up spreading all over the grass, choking and smothering the other flowers.

'OK, look,' said Ella. 'You're all good at

your magic but you have to learn to control it.'

'Why don't we show you how to do it?' I said. I pointed at the twig that Lizzie had made smoke. 'Fire be with me.' The twig burst into flame. I concentrated on it and the fire grew into a tall column shape reaching up and up . . .

'Fire be gone!' I snapped and the fire died. I turned to Lizzie. 'You need to be able to control the fire. Find the strength to make something burn and then control it with your mind.'

'And if you make things grow you must control them,' said Ella to Isabella. 'Like this. Grow anew!' she murmured, pointing to the buttercups. They shot up tall. 'Be gone!' whispered Ella and they shrank back down until there was just a small patch left. After that, Faye conjured a rain cloud, but in the blink of an eye she had changed the rain to sleet and then hail and then snow before making it rain again and finally making it vanish. And then Allegra conjured a breeze that whispered through the clearing before building up to a wind and then disappearing when she snapped her fingers.

'See!' she said. 'Easy!'

The younger spirits exchanged looks. I felt a bit sorry for them. We had made it look so easy for them but I knew how hard we had all found it to control our magic when we had first become stardust spirits.

'You just need to practise loads,' I tried to encourage them. 'It will get easier. Why don't we pair up? Georgia, you go with Faye; Charlotte with Allegra; Isabella with Ella, and Lizzie, you come with me.'

We went off in our twos but practising the magic wasn't a great success.

Lizzie just couldn't get the branches I found for her to do more than heat up and smoke.

'Oh, why can't I make them burst into flames?' she sighed.

'Keep trying,' I told her. 'You've just got to really believe you can do it. I'm sure you're almost there. Look, try imagining throwing a fireball. That's how I did it at first.'

Lizzie threw out her hand. 'Fire be with me!' But nothing happened. 'Oh!' she exclaimed, looking like she wanted to stamp her foot.

Behind me I could hear Ella talking to Isabella. 'No, Isabella, you've got to make it smaller.' I glanced round; Isabella had just grown a giant rose bush. 'Look, like this!' Ella said, shrinking it back to normal size. 'It's easy.'

'But what are you doing? How are you doing it? I don't get it!' said Isabella, looking frustrated.

'Neither do I!' said Charlotte, overhearing. She was working with Allegra. 'I just can't change the strength of the wind.'

Opposite them, Faye and Georgia were arguing because Georgia just couldn't get it to rain in the clearing. She could conjure a rain cloud but it wouldn't go anywhere she wanted.

'You just have to think what you want it to do,' said Faye.

'I *am* doing!' said Georgia.

I turned to Lizzie. 'Why don't you try again?' I said encouragingly.

Lizzie put out her hand. 'Fire be with me!' For a moment I thought I saw a spark fly towards the branch she was pointing out but it disappeared before it reached it.

'Oh, I can't do this!' Lizzie cried. 'I just can't make it burst into flames.'

'You're just not trying hard enough,' Faye told her.

'I so am!' retorted Lizzie.

'You can't be,' Faye said. 'Otherwise you'd be able to do it.'

Lizzie glared at her. 'What do you know? You're not even a summer spirit.'

'No, but I've been a stardust spirit a lot longer than you!' said Faye. 'You need to practise more and try harder.'

'Well, I'm fed up of practising.' Lizzie flew up in the air. 'Come on,' she called to Georgia, Charlotte and Isabella. 'I've had enough of this. Let's go!'

'You can't go. You're supposed to be practising with us,' Ella protested, looking shocked.

'We've practised,' said Charlotte. 'I'm fed up too. Let's play tag!' She swooped up to join Lizzie.

The other two joined them and they all swooped away.

'Well,' said Ella, putting her hands on her hips. 'I can't believe that.'

'Oh, let them go,' Allegra said. 'It wasn't much fun for us either. At least we can go and check on the deer now.'

I nodded. 'Come on!'

We flew into the air. A little way off to

the
east I
could hear
the younger
girls laughing as
they played tag. In a
way they reminded me of
how we'd been when we'd
first become stardust spirits.
Everything was so new and exciting; they
had so much to learn and so much they
couldn't do yet. I remembered what
Xanthe had said: *You'll have to be patient
and help them learn how to do it for
themselves.*

Then I felt a bit guilty. We hadn't really
been helping *them* learn, we'd been
showing them what *we* could do.

Before I could think any more about it, Allegra pointed downwards. 'Look, there are some deer!'

A group of fallow deer were lying on the ground in the shelter of a copse of trees. They had chestnut-brown coats with white spots, and pale legs and tummies. They were all lying down but if you are looking for them in the evening or in the day they can be difficult to find because their spotted coats are such a good camouflage. If they stand very still, they seem to merge into the trees and sometimes you only spot them when you see an ear flicking.

'It's a group of females,' said Allegra.

I nodded. Male deer are larger and have big antlers at this time of year.

'Look at the fawns!' said Faye.

There were eight baby deer curled up with their mothers. Even the oldest looked like it was only about two months old. They were very cute. I looked at the does without fawns. Eight of them had big stomachs and looked as if they were pregnant.

'We should go and get Xanthe,' said Ella.

'We don't need to all go,' said Faye. 'Why don't you and I go, Ella?'

'We'll try and find the stags while you're gone,' said Allegra. 'They will probably be somewhere fairly close by.'

Ella and Faye hurried off. 'Should we go and look over there?' Allegra said, pointing through the trees. But just then one of the does heaved herself up. She had a big belly. She looked round at her sides, her ears flicking.

'She looks very pregnant,' I commented.

Allegra nodded. The deer walked towards some trees, stopped and pawed at the ground. She seemed very restless. Allegra watched her thoughtfully. 'You know, I think she might be about to have her baby now.'

'Oh wow!' I gasped. I'd never seen an animal giving birth in real life before.

We flew after the doe. She headed out of the copse and across a clearing. She walked restlessly, her tail swishing. Every so often she would turn and look at her flanks. After about five minutes, she disappeared into a thick cluster of rowan trees at the side of the clearing and we saw her lie down.

'How long will it take?' I asked Allegra.

'Probably quite a while. Why don't we leave her for now while she gets settled and go and check on the stags? We can come back in ten minutes and see how she's doing.'

It took longer than ten minutes to find the stags but eventually we came across them among the oak and horse chestnut trees. They were very beautiful with long antlers, big dark eyes and delicate faces. 'There's eleven of them,' said Allegra, counting them. 'And they all look healthy. We can tell Xanthe they're here if she wants to look at them.'

'Let's go back to the pregnant doe now,' I said eagerly.

We flew back. 'Do you think Faye and Ella will be back yet?' I asked.

Allegra shook her head. 'No, they had

to get back to the stardust clearing, find out where Xanthe is, go and find her and then come back here. It'll take them a while, I reckon.'

Suddenly I heard the sound of voices ahead of us. There were people in the clearing. The voices seem to be coming from up in the air so I knew it had to be other stardust spirits.

'Come on, Charlotte! Make it really windy!' I heard Lizzie's call.

'OK,' came Charlotte's voice. 'Here goes! Then you can practise your magic!'

'It's Lizzie and the others,' I said to Allegra.

'They're going to disturb the doe,' Allegra said.

'They don't know she's there,' I said. 'Quick! Let's go and tell them!'

'It's my turn!' I heard Lizzie shout. 'I'm really going to do it this time!'

As Allegra and I flew into the clearing, I caught my breath. Lizzie had her hands raised and she was facing a branch on the floor. There was a look of real determination on her face. 'Fire be with me!' She threw her hands down and a ball of fire erupted from her fingers. It shot past the twig she had been aiming at and crashed into the ground beside the rowan trees. Lizzie and the others gasped in astonishment. There was a loud whoosh and the dry grass and leaves at the base of the trees exploded into flames.

'No!' I cried as the fire leapt upwards, fanned and caught by the wind that Charlotte had conjured a minute earlier.

The younger spirits heard my voice and swung round, alarm on their faces.

'There's a deer having a baby in those trees!' Allegra shouted.

'A deer?' Lizzie echoed in dismay.

'Oh no!' gasped Isabella.

The heavy grey smoke was filling the air. The fire had reached the tree's branches and was crackling loudly; bits of burning bark spitting into the dark sky.

'Quick, Georgia!' I shouted, flying over and grabbing Georgia's arm. 'Make it rain! Put the fire out!' I coughed as the smoke caught at the back of my throat.

Allegra was already snapping her fingers to stop the wind that was making the fire burn stronger. I wished I could do that to the fire, but fires are different. Once they catch hold and start burning things up they have a life of their own and can't be stopped except by the person who started them.

'Ow!' Lizzie cried out as a piece of burning bark caught her arm.

'Hurry up, Georgia!' I cried.

'Rain be with me!' Georgia gasped, pointing at the rowan trees. A rain cloud

formed to one side of her and rain began
to pour down but it wasn't close enough
to the fire. Georgia tried again but this
time the rain cloud formed on the other
side of the clearing.

'I–I can't do it!' she stammered. 'I can't
get the rain to go where I want.'

I shot my hand out. 'Rain be with me!'
I begged.

I felt the magic surge up inside me.
I tried to control it, to hang on to it so I
could use it to make a rain cloud come,
but before I could do anything it had
slipped away like bathwater through my
fingers.

'Lucy!' Allegra shouted desperately. She
was dodging through the smoke, trying to
peer down through the flames. 'The deer
can't get up. She's started having the baby!'

I felt sick. The doe and her baby could die in there. There had to be something we could do. My mind raced over every bit of stardust magic that I knew and had ever used. I'd done so much stuff on my own, so much with the others . . .

With the others!

The thought yelled out in my head. *Of course!* Stardust magic was at its strongest when people worked together. I might not be able to make it rain myself but maybe if Georgia and I worked together – if we used her ability to make a rain cloud and my experience of controlling and using magic . . .

I didn't know if it would work but I had to try. 'Georgia!' I cried. 'Let's work together. If you make the rain cloud, I'll try and help you direct it over the fire.'

She looked at me in confusion. There wasn't time to explain more. When I'd been in Wales, Tess and I had worked summer magic together, holding hands, reading each other's thoughts and combining our magic powers. I'd never tried to work magic with a different kind of spirit before but now I had stardust from all four Royal Stars maybe I *could* do it.

'Lucy!' Allegra shouted above the crackle and roar of the fire. 'The flames are getting closer!'

'Please do something!' begged Lizzie.

I didn't stop to think any longer. I grabbed Georgia's hands. 'We're going to do this together,' I said. 'I'll help you.' She looked scared and worried. 'You can do this.' I tried to sound calm. 'Just trust me.

Close your eyes.' I shut out the noise of the flames, the crackling, the shouts from the others. I felt magic surge up inside me, powerful and strong. *I'm here*, I thought, trying to reach Georgia with my mind.

Lucy? I heard her thoughts faintly.

Yes, I replied in my head. *I'm here. I'm with you. I'm going to help you.* I gripped her fingers tightly and felt her relax slightly. *Can you conjure a rain cloud?*

Yes.

I felt my hands tingling as she called on her magic. I could feel her concentrating.

'Rain be with me,' I heard her whisper.

Power surged between us, moving from her to me and back again. I felt raindrops on my skin and looked up. There was a rain cloud above us. Suddenly, I felt the magic getting stronger and Georgia start to tense and panic.

I concentrated hard and took hold of the power. Holding it, containing it while Georgia used it to keep the rain cloud there.

It's all right, I reassured Georgia. *I've got control of it. Help me move it. You can do it. You just have to believe you can.*

I felt her focus again and we concentrated on the rain cloud. It moved towards the fire.

'You've done it!' Allegra gasped as it reached the flames. The rain poured down. As the fire sizzled and spat and then died away, Allegra sent a curling wind to sweep away the smoke, controlling the wind so that it didn't fan the flames.

'The fire's going out!' exclaimed Charlotte.

We all watched in relief as the flames died. Lizzie was clutching her arm where the bark had burnt her. 'How's the deer?' she asked anxiously.

Allegra swooped down into the trees. 'Not good,' she called. 'She's really stressed.'

The rest of us flew down to join her. The smell of burnt wood was strong among the rowan trees and there were wisps of smoke still floating through the air. The deer was lying down, panting for breath, her eyes wide and terrified. She kicked at the ground with her back legs. Her sides were heaving. I could tell she wanted to get up and run away but it was too late. I could see the tips of the fawn's hooves under her tail – the birth had started.

'Can't you do anything?' Isabella asked, looking at me.

I shook my head. I longed to. But the deer needed calming and neither me nor Allegra had any magic that could do it.

'I wish Xanthe was here,' said Allegra, biting her lip.

'We didn't realize the deer was in the trees,' said Lizzie looking at the terrified doe. 'I would never have . . .' Her voice choked and tears welled in her eyes. 'Oh, Lucy, what's going to happen? Is she going to die?'

'She'll be all right.' I desperately hoped I was right.

Suddenly I heard a familiar voice in

the clearing. 'What's happened here?'

'Xanthe!' Relief flooded through me. I flew out of the trees.

Xanthe was hovering in the clearing with Ella and Faye.

'What's going on?' she demanded, looking at the burnt trees.

There wasn't time to explain. 'Come quick!' I urged. 'There's a deer here. She's having her baby but she's terrified. Please! Just come!' As Xanthe flew over I quickly gabbled out what had happened. Faye and Ella followed us into the trees.

The others were watching the deer anxiously. She was kicking and struggling to get up.

'Stay calm,' Allegra was saying desperately. 'It's OK. The fire's gone.'

Lizzie was crying.

Faye flew over and put her arm round her. 'Are you OK?' she demanded, looking at the burn on Lizzie's arm.

'Don't worry about me, it's the deer,' sobbed Lizzie. 'Look at her, Faye! What if something goes wrong with the birth? What if she dies? It'll be all my fault. Oh, Faye!' She buried her face in her sister's shoulder.

'It's OK, Lizzie. I think I might be able to sort this out,' Xanthe said quickly. She landed next to the animal. The doe kicked out with her legs but Xanthe quickly laid a soothing hand on her neck and closing her eyes began to move her lips. She spoke so softly to her that I couldn't hear what she was saying but gradually the doe began to stop panicking, the fear left her eyes and her

body relaxed. Xanthe stroked her head.
The deer's sides heaved still but there was
less of a panicky motion to them. She
licked Xanthe's hand, groaned deeply and
laid her head on the grass. Xanthe
stroked her cheek.

'I've told her that there is nothing to
be scared of,' Xanthe said to us. 'She is

calm now and I think she will have her baby without problems.'

Lizzie cried harder and Faye hugged her. Allegra flew over and hugged me too.

'The baby's coming,' Xanthe said softly, looking at the deer's heaving sides. 'Let's watch and see what happens.'

An hour later, a damp baby fawn was standing on wobbly legs, feeding from his mum, his tiny brown tail wagging. It had been amazing watching the birth. I've seen animals being born on TV but I've never actually watched one in real life before. With the doe now calm, the fawn was born very easily. He came out in a kind of see-through white sack. The doe cleaned it off him and licked him all over until he raised his head and made a bleating noise. Then she nudged him with her nose and gradually he tried to stand on his long thin wobbly legs. It was like watching Bambi! He kept half getting up and then falling over. It was so tempting to help him but Xanthe said he had to get up on his own. Finally he stood up and then a few minutes later began to feed.

'He's gorgeous,' said Allegra.

'And very healthy,' said Xanthe, looking pleased.

'And the mother deer is OK too?' Georgia asked.

'Yes, soon they will rejoin the other females,' Xanthe said.

'I'm so glad you got here when you did,' Allegra told her. 'It was awful – not being able to do anything.'

'I felt like that when the fire started,' said Lizzie. 'I was so glad when you and Lucy arrived, Allegra, and I knew you'd be able to help.'

Xanthe smiled at her. 'We all help each other in the stardust world. We are stronger when we work together using our different skills and abilities.'

Georgia glanced shyly at me. 'Like when you helped me move the rain cloud. I'd never have been able to do it without you.'

'But I couldn't have made it rain on my own,' I said.

Ella looked at Isabella. 'And you can help me regrow all the burnt plants now.'

Isabella nodded eagerly.

'Here,' Faye said to Lizzie. 'Let me see your burn.'

She looked at it and then gently held her hand over the red, blistered patch of skin on Lizzie's arm. Lizzie gasped as the blisters healed and the redness faded. 'Wow! I didn't know you could do magic like that!' she said, looking very impressed.

'Faye's very good at working healing magic,' said Xanthe.

'That's so amazing,' said Lizzie. 'Oh, Faye, I'm sorry I said you didn't know anything before and I'm sorry we all took off like that. We should have listened to you and stayed and practised.'

'That's OK,' said Faye.

'We were too bossy,' I said. 'And we showed you what we could do too much; we weren't very good at helping you.

Maybe we can try again. If you want to, of course?' I said, looking round at the younger spirits.

'Yes, please!' they all chorused.

Xanthe smiled. 'I'll leave you all to it then.'

'Look!' Faye said suddenly. The doe and her fawn were leaving the trees. He

trotted along beside her, swaying slightly on his unsteady legs. We watched them disappear back into the trees to join the other deer where they belonged.

'Come on, let's regrow the plants,' Ella said to Isabella.

'And we can play tag while you do,' declared Allegra. She swooped at Lizzie. 'Tag!'

Laughing and shouting we all raced into the air.

So, all in all it was a really cool night. It could have all turned out really badly, but it didn't. The deer and her fawn were OK and, later on, we started helping the younger spirits with their magic again and got on loads better. Faye and Lizzie hardly argued at all! We're all going to go and see the deer again tomorrow night –

well, apart from Allegra. She'll be in
Dorset with Xanthe. It'll be weird
without her but she's going to phone and
I'll tell her what we've been doing.

   Night for now!

Friday 10.15 a.m.

Allegra and Xanthe left this morning.
I've never been to Dorset. I wonder what
animals they have there. Xanthe said that
Chloe lives on the coast by the beach. A
bit like Tess in Wales. I've been thinking
about the dolphin that Tess saved and all
the animals we have come across in our
woods. There are so many amazing
animals in the wild. I'm going to tell you
a few facts about some of my favourites.

Dormice

What they look like

They look a bit like a cross between a
hamster and a mouse. They have a golden

coat, big black eyes and a long furry tail. They get really fat in the autumn just before they hibernate for the winter.

What they eat

Flowers, pollen, insects, nuts – especially hazelnuts. They open hazelnuts by gnawing a round hole in one side to get the nut kernel out. If you find a hazelnut shell with a round hole in it then it might mean there are dormice nearby.

Where they live

They live in woods and hedges. The dormice in our woods live in a hazel grove. They like trees with sprawling branches so they can run along them and not have to go on the ground. They don't like living in very dark, shady areas with tall trees. They like clearings with light and lots of different shrubs.

What they are like

They are usually very shy but when I've been a stardust spirit they have come and sat on my hands and let me cuddle them. They have very soft coats and their whiskers twitch a lot. When I first became a stardust spirit I saved one from a fire. I didn't realize it was a dormouse until after the fire had been put out. It was brilliant because it meant that builders weren't allowed to build houses on the land where the dormice lived. Dormice are an endangered species.

Other facts

They are very rarely seen; they are nocturnal, which means they are active at night. They live up to five years old – much older than most mice.

Honey Buzzards

What they look like

They are large birds of prey with broad wings and a long tail. They are very beautiful and majestic. They have greyish-brown feathers on their upper bodies, brown, black and white feathers on their wings and white feathers on their tummies and chests. Their bills are long and curved. We had two honey buzzards nesting in our woods. We called them Bob and Wendy. We had to protect them from some teenagers who wanted to steal their eggs. Luckily we managed it and Bob and Wendy had three healthy chicks.

What they eat
Mainly insect larvae – particularly wasps and bees. Imagine eating something like

that! They have very heavily scaled legs and feet, and scales around their beak to protect them from stings.

Where they live

They live in forests and woods.

What they are like

They are shy and secretive and easily disturbed. They fly silently. Both the mum and the dad sit on the eggs.

Other facts

They are very rare and their nests have to be kept secret because of egg collectors. Xanthe says there are only about sixty breeding pairs in the UK.

Otters

What they look like

They look a little like a cross between a dog and a very small sea lion. They have cheeky black eyes, mid-brown coats the colour of milk chocolate and creamy-white underbellies. Their fur is sleek and thick. Male otters can be about 1.2 metres long from their nose to their tail. Females are a bit smaller.

What they eat
Mainly fish but also frogs and small birds.

Where they live
Along the banks of rivers and lakes and on the sea coasts. They each have their own territory and in that territory might have many different resting places. These resting places are called holts. Otters sometimes use old rabbit burrows or badger setts or nest in the roots of trees or in log piles. We had to help create holts out of logs to encourage otters to come back to the woods.

What they are like
Very cheeky! They like playing. There are otters near the river in the wood and their cubs love playing games. They chase

each other around and play fight. In the winter we saw some sliding down a snowy bank!

Other facts

They live for about five years in the wild. The cubs stay with their mothers for over a year. They are nocturnal so come out at night. There used to be lots of otters in the UK but they are much rarer now and they are also heavily protected.

Saturday 3.00 a.m.

It was quiet in the woods tonight without Allegra. I hope she's having a fun time. Maybe she'll find out tonight if Chloe is a stardust spirit or not. We played hide-and-seek again and went to check on the firecrests. Their eggs are still all fine. I wonder when they will hatch? Faye and Ella tried to help me practise my winter and spring magic. I think I'm getting better at growing things. I managed to grow some ivy over one of the otter holts which should help disguise it. I also managed to conjure a small rain cloud tonight but it disappeared almost straight away!

Oh well, I guess I have to just keep on trying! Bed now. I'll write more in the morning.

Saturday 10.00 a.m.

Hi again,

I haven't got much to do today. It's always
boring when Allegra's away. At least she'll
be back tomorrow. Last night Ella
suggested that I draw some animal tracks
for you. We all love looking at animal
tracks and working out what animal
made them. And it's something you can
do in the day even when you're not a
stardust spirit!

Here are some pictures of the tracks
different animals make.

Dog		Cat	
Badger		Fox	
Otter		Mole	
Hedgehog		Shrew	
Mouse		Weasel	

I hope that if you're in the countryside or the woods you find some tracks and manage to work out what animal made them! OK, I'd better go and clean out Thumper. More later!

Sunday 3.15 a.m.

Back again now. We took Lizzie, Georgia, Charlotte and Isabella to see different bits of the woods where endangered animals live. We showed them the otters by the river, the firecrests (the eggs have all hatched!), the dormice and the blue-backed beetles (the MOST boring animals in the world – Allegra and I once had to spend three days counting them!). Then we all went looking for great crested newts in the three ponds in the woods. Xanthe says she thinks they might return soon. They look a bit like small lizards that live in water. They're not very pretty but you can't just help animals that are cute. After that we all practised our magic and I managed to make it rain properly. I wish Allegra had been there to see but I'll show her when she gets back. I can't wait to tell her about the firecrest eggs too!

Sunday 2.00 p.m.

Allegra's home! She's just rung me. I'm going over there for the afternoon. She says she's got loads to tell me! Apparently Chloe *is* a stardust spirit!

Sunday 6.00 p.m.

Wow! When Allegra said she had lots to tell me, she was right. She and Xanthe arrived in Dorset Friday afternoon. She said that Chloe lives in a village in a terraced house near the beach with her mum and dad. Neither of her parents are stardust spirits and she'd never heard about stardust (just like me) but Xanthe told her about it as if it was a story. As soon as the stars came out and her parents were in bed, Chloe told Allegra that she wanted to try. She turned into a stardust spirit straight away!

Xanthe was really pleased and she and Allegra told Chloe all about the stardust world. However, the bad news for Chloe is that the nearest group of stardust spirits meet at a beach a long way away from her home and Xanthe thinks it will be too far for Chloe to fly every night so she's going to have to be a stardust spirit on her own although Xanthe's going to try and find out if there are any other stardust spirits nearby. Being on your own would be so weird! I think part of the fun is doing magic with friends and working with other people.

Allegra said that Xanthe is very worried about it. She's told Chloe that she and Allegra will go back and visit her as much as they can while Chloe learns how to use her magic and Chloe is going to phone and email them if she has any questions. She's also going to come and stay with Allegra and Xanthe in a few weeks' time and see everyone here. It'll be fun to meet her.

The place where Chloe lives sounds lovely. Allegra says it's really wild and beautiful with steep cliffs. There is hardly any sand; it's mainly pebbles. She showed me some weird stones she'd collected on the beach. They're called hagstones and they've got a hole right through the middle, like a Polo!

Xanthe came in just as Allegra was showing them to me. She told me that hagstones are really magical. In the old days, people used them to keep witches away and to cast spells. Xanthe told me that some stardust spirits use them when they are trying to work weather magic. At first I thought she was talking

about normal autumn and winter
magic and I was surprised because
no stardust spirits I've ever met have
used stones to help them. But Xanthe
wasn't talking about that kind of
magic. Weather magic is when you
change the weather for everyone in a
large area, like over a whole town;
it's not just making one rain cloud
or a gust of wind like winter and
autumn spirits do normally. It's a
type of deep magic that only a few
stardust spirits can do. Xanthe says
that stardust spirits who can work
weather magic are born with the
ability to do it.

I thought it sounded pretty cool and
then Xanthe told me something even
cooler! Stardust spirits who can work

weather magic always love horses. It's because the weather is actually controlled by magical cloud horses who live in the skies! It's true! I could hardly believe it but it is. Xanthe said that these horses can't be seen by normal people, but they are there in the clouds all the time. The stallions who lead the herds are proud, brave and powerful and can never be forced to do things. Stardust spirits with the gift of weather magic use hagstones to communicate with them and work with them to change the weather.

As soon as Xanthe told me, I thought about how brilliant it would be to be able to see cloud horses. Xanthe says no one has ever been up into the cloud horses' kingdom but just imagine what it would be like! To stroke a cloud horse, to sit on its back, to fly with it through the air . . . WOW!

Oh goodness. I've just seen the time. I've been writing for ages. I'm supposed to be going back round to Allegra's to sleep over. We're going to turn ourselves into stardust spirits as

soon as it gets dark. There's loads we
want to do tonight – see the firecrest
chicks, look for pipistrelle bats, which
are another endangered species, play a
new game called magic stuck-in-the-
mud that Allegra's just thought up, and
I want to practise my winter magic
some more.

I can't believe that I've almost filled
the pages of this diary now. It feels like
so much has happened since I started
writing about my stardust world for
you. I hope you've enjoyed reading
about it all! As a stardust spirit, they say
you get a special sense about other
people with enough stardust in them to
be a spirit and, you know what, I have a
really strong feeling that if you are
reading this, you might well have

enough stardust too. How exciting
would that be? Just remember what you
have to do . . .

Lots of love,

Lucy xxx

P.S. Always believe in magic. It does exist
– it REALLY does.

Discover magical new worlds with
Linda Chapman

The Circle of
Secrets & Magic
lindachapman.co.uk

✦ **Gallop** with the unicorns at Unicorn Meadows

✦ **Fly** with the magical spirits of Stardust Forest

✦ **Swim** through Mermaid Falls with Electra and her friends

✦ **Play** with new friends at Unicorn School

With great **activities**, gorgeous **downloads**, games galore and an exciting new online fanzine!

What are you waiting for?
The magic begins at

lindachapman.co.uk

puffin.co.uk

Stardust

I believe in stardust,
I believe in stardust,
I believe in stardust!

During the day Lucy is a normal ten-year-old girl, but every night she whispers the words of the stardust spell and magically becomes a stardust spirit . . .

Discover the magical world of stardust!

lindachapman.co.uk

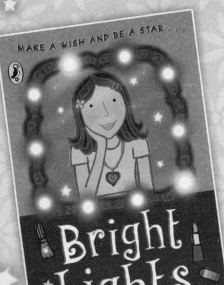
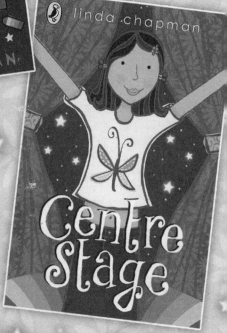